Dan Blank

For Izzy...

Because she always makes me happy

Thigpen McThwacket
What a melodious name
For a remarkable chap
Of melodious fame

Such an incredible lad
Was Thigpen McThwacket
That he made by himself
An incredible racket

From the very first instant
This fine lad was born
He had a fantastic talent
For playing the horn

And this music he made
Inspired his mind
To be the best music-maker
The best of all time

23

But Thigpen soon found
The horn wasn't enough
So he began adding
More other stuff

He strapped two cymbals
Inside of his knees
Which made a loud bang
Whenever he pleased

With a horn to go toot
And a cymbal to bang
He put a bell on his belt
Which he frequently rang

With toots and bangs
And even more rings
Thigpen now wanted
Even more things

So he tied a harmonica
Onto the end of his nose
Which made a sweet hum
Whenever he chose

From miles and miles
People would come
To see McThwacket
Toot, ring, bang, and hum

They'd listen for hours
To the incredible racket
That could only be made
By Thigpen McThwacket

They cheered and they hollered
As the one-man band played
And longer he did
The longer they stayed

"Thigpen McThwacket,"
The townspeople chanted
"We all love your racket,"
They raved and they ranted

"Your racket is lovely
But what more can you do?"
So next to his horn
He put a kazoo

With a toot and a bang
A ring and a hum
A kazoo going quack
Made more people come

This should be plenty
To please the whole town
Thigpen decided
As he marched up and down

But unright he was
In fact he was wrong
They wanted even more sounds
To add to his song

"We all love your racket
And the quack of kazoo,
But Thigpen McThwacket
What more can you do?"

So with a toot and a bang
A ring, quack, and a hum
Onto his chest
He strapped a large drum

thud, toot, and ring
quack, hum, and a bang
hat should be plenty
o please the whole gang

"A drum! A drum!"
The townspeople yelled
"It's thunderous thud
Sounds great with the bell!"

Yes the drum sounded fine
But it weighed quite a lot
The townsfolk were happy
But Thigpen was not

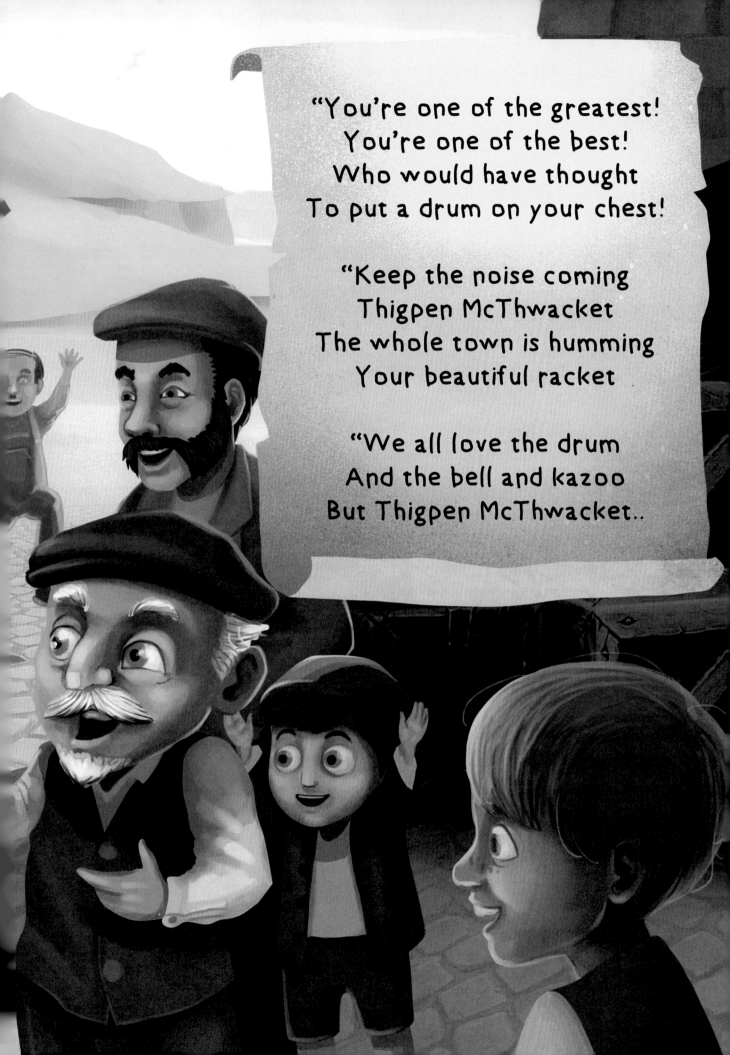

"You're one of the greatest!
You're one of the best!
Who would have thought
To put a drum on your chest!

"Keep the noise coming
Thigpen McThwacket
The whole town is humming
Your beautiful racket

"We all love the drum
And the bell and kazoo
But Thigpen McThwacket..

"What more can you do?"

"What more could they want,"
The tired man wondered
As his achy knees ached
And his big new drum thundered

"I've got cymbals, a bell
A horn and kazoo
A drum and a hum
But what else can I do?"

Without missing a beat
Right next to his drum
He put a guitar
For one hand to strum

"Now I'm complete
This has to be all
Any more stuff
And I surely will fall"

"Just look at him now!"
The townspeople shouted
And more people came
As the crowd became crowded

"Would you believe it
He's got a guitar
Now that is the best
The best sound by far!

"You're brilliant McThwacket!
You're one of a kind
Just one more sound
And you're the best of all time!"

At first the townsfolk
Let out a moan
But then began shouting
Thoughts of their own

"Stuff a big tuba,
Way up in your nose,
Which would trumpet triumphant
When your tuba nose blows

"Or a little blue flute
Inside of your ear
Which would play a sweet song
Whenever you hear

"Or if you have room
Inside of your socks
Put an oboe, a harp
And some new wooden blocks"

Thigpen McThwacket
Was now very upset
One more sound that they want
One more sound they shall get

"Blocks in my socks!
A flute in my ear!
I'll give them a sound
The whole world will hear!

"This sound shall be huge
High, wide and tall
It will please all these people
Please them once and for all!"

Oh, Thigpen was weary
His racket weighed quite a lot
He struggled to budge
His feet from their spot

But Thigpen McThwacket
Had it set in his mind
That he'd be the best
The best of all time

So he took off his hat
And what did he do?
Put on top of his head...
Not one piano...

But two!

Two pianos on top
And a mess down below
Thigpen McThwacket
Was an incredible show!

The townspeople gasped
At Thigpen's surprise
And his incredible racket
Of unforgettable size

"He's truly the greatest!"
The townsfolk declared
As the pianos swayed slowly
High up in the air

But his thin body trembled
His knees began quaking
From bottom to top
McThwacket was shaking

As his skinny legs buckled
He played one last sound
Then McThwacket's great racket
Crashed to the ground

There were blue pieces here
And red parts over there
And they probably fit
But no one knew where

The townspeople laughed
At Thigpen McThwacket
And the super-sized mess
Of his over-sized racket

"You're foolish McThwacket
You're truly a bum
Why all of us knew
You should have stopped
with the drum

"But you didn't listen
To what we all said
That pianos don't fit well
On top of your head"

They all left McThwacket
Alone with his mess
Who was very disheartened
About doing his best

His drum was destroyed
As was the kazoo
And the cymbal and bell
And the other stuff too

But all by itself
Which McThwacket soon saw
Was his favorite horn
It survived the great fall

Did he find the horn?
Or did the horn find the boy?
Whatever the case
In the horn he found joy

So he picked up his horn
And he started to play
And he played and he played
Yes he played every day

And shortly thereafter
The townspeople came back
Though there wasn't a thud
A ring, hum, or quack

There was only the toot
Of a beautiful horn
And from that one single sound
A legend was born

You see Thigpen McThwacket
Became one of a kind
The very best horn player
The best of all time.

-THE END-

Made in the USA
Middletown, DE
19 June 2017